My Father's Hands

by Joanne Ryder

illustrated by Mark Graham

Morrow Junior Books
New York

For Raymond Ryder and Arthur Charpentier,
treasured fathers who nurtured their daughters with love
—J. R.

To Katie and Oscar
—M. G.

Wild animals should always be handled with great care and adult supervision.

Oil on Strathmore bristol paper was used for the full-color artwork.
The text type is 21-point Goudy Bold.

Text copyright © 1994 by Joanne Ryder
Illustrations copyright © 1994 by Mark Graham

Library of Congress Cataloging-in-Publication Data
Ryder, Joanne.
My father's hands / Joanne Ryder; illustrated by Mark Graham.
p. cm.
Summary: A child's father digs in the garden, finding and presenting for inspection such wonders
as a round gold beetle and a leaf-green mantis.
ISBN 0-688-09189-X (trade) — ISBN 0-688-09190-3 (library)
[1. Fathers and child—Fiction. 2. Gardening—Fiction. 3. Insects—Fiction.]
I. Graham, Mark, ill. II. Title.
PZ7.R9752My 1994 [E]—dc20 93-27116 CIP AC

My father's hands
are big and strong,
scooping up earth
and lifting
sacks of seeds.

Thin cracks
run down
my father's fingers.
Dirt fills
every line
and edges
each nail black.

Planting,
watering,
weeding,
my father's hands
shape a patch
of earth
into our garden.

From the porch
I watch him,
kneeling in the sun,
reaching into shadows
to find something
small and hidden.

He calls to me
with a promise
in his voice,
and I run, seeing
his hands curl
like a flower
budding, then
unfolding wide
so I can see . . .

the pink circle of worm,

the round beetle
shining in gold armor,

the snail sliding
over the dark cracks,

or the leaf-green mantis
balancing today
on long thin legs.

I bend closer,
knowing that
nothing within
my father's hands
will harm me.

Gently my father
tips his hands,
softly urging
the small one
to my open palms.
Green prickly feet
find their footing
on my steady fingers.

The mantis tilts
his pointed face,
his huge round eyes
watching me
watch him.
He is so light,
so bold, so strange.
I wonder what
he thinks of me,
of my hands
soft and warm.

And when
he thinks
I'm dreaming,
he leaps—
scampering
up my arm,
hanging
and swaying
on my shirt.

My father
plucks
the traveler free
and gives
him back to me.

His hands
surrounding mine,
we take
the small one
to his bush,
watch him
till he melts
green in the greenness.

No one will
ever bring
me better
treasures
than the ones
cupped
in my father's hands.

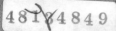